This book belongs to:

....

For rainbow seekers,
dinosaur hunters, and
every kind of family.

First published in 2024 by

Crocodile Books
An imprint of Interlink Publishing Group, Inc.
46 Crosby Street
Northampton, Massachusetts 01060
www.interlinkbooks.com

Published simultaneously in Great Britain in 2024 by Hodder Children's Books,
an imprint of Hachette Children's Group

Library of Congress cataloging-in-publication data available:

ISBN 978-1-62371-700-1

MIX
Paper from
responsible sources
FSC® C104740
FSC
www.fsc.org

10 9 8 7 6 5 4 3 2 1

Printed in China

RAINBOW SAURUS

Steve Antony

Crocodile
Books, USA

"We're following a rainbow
to find the **Rainbowsaurus**.
We're following a rainbow.
Would you like to join us?"

"**Moo,**" said the red cow.
And off they marched together.

Moo

Moo

"**Rainbowsaurus,** where are you?"

"We're following a rainbow
to find the **Rainbowsaurus**.
We're following a rainbow.
Who would like to join us?"

"**Hiss,**" said the orange snake.
"**Ribbit,**" said the yellow frog.

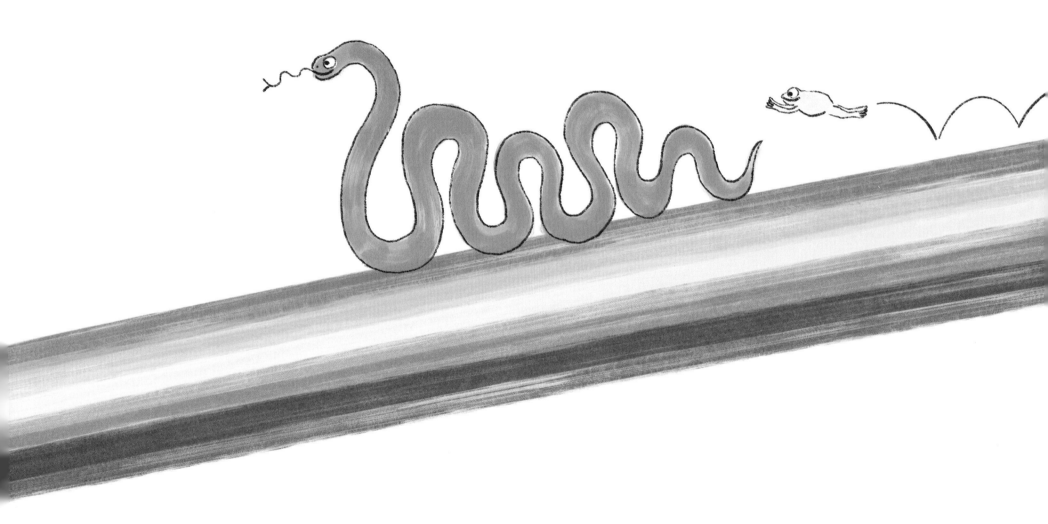

And off they marched together.

Ribbit

Hiss

Moo

Hiss

Ribbit

Hiss

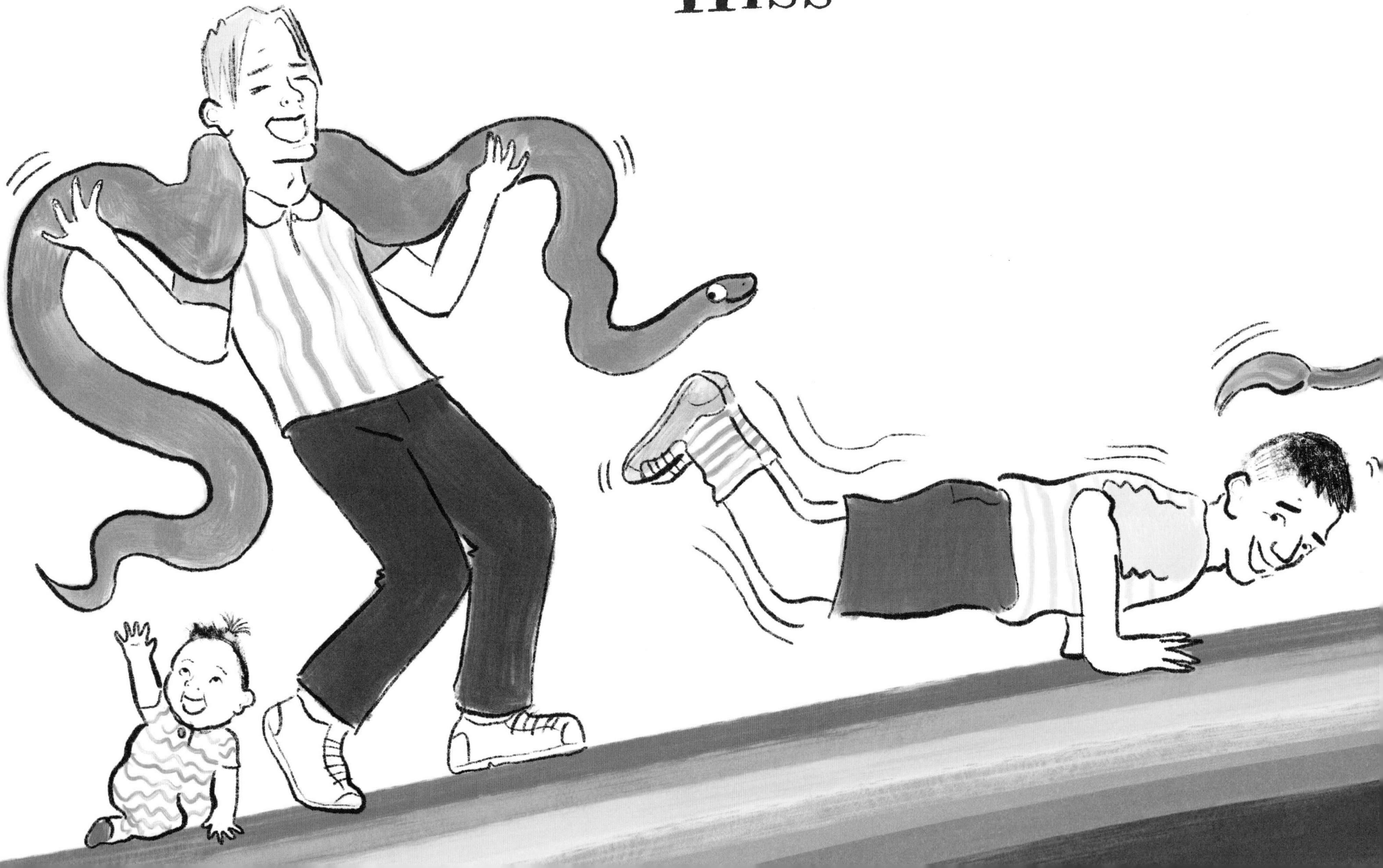

Moo

"**Rainbowsaurus,** where are you?"

"We're following a rainbow
to find the **Rainbowsaurus**.
We're following a rainbow.
Won't you come and join us?"

"**Oink,**" said the green pig.
"**Growl,**" said the indigo bear.
"**Gobble,**" said the violet turkey.
And off they marched together.

Moo

"**Rainbowsaurus,** where are you?"

"We're following a rainbow.
Come along and join us.
We're following a rainbow
to find the **Rainbowsaurus**."

"**Quack,**" said the black duck.
"**Buzz,**" said the brown bee.
"**Baa,**" said the blue sheep.
"**Hee-haw,**" said the pink donkey.
"**Cock-a-doodle-doo,**" said the white rooster.
And off they marched together.

Ribbit

Hiss

Baa

Buzz

Hee-haw

Moo

Growl

Gobble

Quack

Oink

Cock-a-doodle-doo

"Rainbowsaurus,

where are **YOU?**"

"**I'm right behind you,**"
said the Rainbowsaurus.

ROAR!

Then off they marched together . . .

Roar Ribbit Gobble Quack Cock-a-doodle-doo

"RAINBOWSAURUS . . .

. . . we love you."